RENSAL THE REDBIT

RENSAL THE REDBIT
A Psychoanalytic Fairy Tale

Eugene J. Mahon

With illustrations by Alice Rowan

KARNAC

First published in 2015 by
Karnac Books Ltd
118 Finchley Road
London NW3 5HT

British Library Cataloguing in Publication Data

A C.I.P. for this book is available from the British Library

ISBN-13: 978-1-78220-188-5

Typeset by V Publishing Solutions Pvt Ltd., Chennai, India

Printed in Great Britain

www.karnacbooks.com

Many years ago in Mytherranea, before the stars had names, when daisies were still called days' eyes, and the moon stayed up all night to keep the darkness company, there lived a race called redbits. Mytherranea was so far to the East that some believed it was always the first to wake the sun in the morning. The redbits were not unlike our rabbits except that they were smaller and stayed small for much longer. There were grown-up redbits, of course, who were big, but the young redbits grew so slowly they could not imagine ever being big. Redbits loved to play in the grass. They ran around like flames dancing between the green columns and this was how they got their name. "There's a red-bit," someone would shout, as if the grass had suddenly changed color. This mistake was repeated often and the name stuck (the world is probably full of colorful mistakes like these that nobody remembers anymore). The redbits had personal names too, of course, names such as Ludik and Silitar. But the redbit I want to tell you about was called Rensal.

One day, Rensal was running through the grass like one solitary red thread amongst many green, when he would have run headlong into the tallest creature he had ever run into if its shadow had not warned him ahead of time.

Rensal, though small, had a brave streak in him and he walked to the end of the shadow and looked up. The tallest creature he had ever seen was looking down. Their eyes met.

The tall one was, of course, a grown-up redbit. Rensal knew from past experience that tall redbits were very different from small redbits, not only in size but also in the way they thought. Rensal knew that if he asked, "Why is your shadow so big and mine so small?" that the tall one would say, "Our shadows depend on how high we are above the ground and how high the sun is in the sky." So he decided not to ask that. Instead, he asked, "Why am I scared of everything bigger than I?"

The Tall One scratched his chin, waiting for a wise expression to appear on his face, and said solemnly, "Your imagination plays tricks on you. You are angry that you are not big, so you believe the big are angry that they are not small."

Rensal knew that if he asked, "What is imagination?" the tall one would say, "It's all the wishes and fears in your mind turned into good pictures and bad pictures." So he decided not to ask that. Instead, he said, "Thank you for helping me. I know I will not be afraid of big things anymore," and he turned on his red heel in the green grass and walked confidently away.

He walked past tall trees and beside tall hills, always under the tall arch of the sky and he was not afraid. Rensal was happy that the big redbit had helped him.

He walked so far and for so long that he did not notice that the sun had climbed down to the lowest rung of the ladder in the sky and that the shadows were longer than ever, even his own. Suddenly, he began to tremble: Rensal afraid of his own shadow!

He ran and ran, back to where he had met the tall one in the grass and was pleased to find him still there. Rensal was short of breath but he gathered his wits and enough wind to blurt out: "I was not afraid until the shadows joined hands and became a solid wall of darkness."

The Tall One scratched his chin, waiting for a wise expression to appear on his face, and said solemnly: "I should have told you about the night. Night is all the shadows in the world gathering together when the sun leaves the sky. They wait patiently in the darkness until the morning birds return with the sun. Then they are free to return again to the daylight things that cast shadows. It is a game that light and shadow have been playing for years."

"But why am I so afraid of it, if it is only a game?" Rensal asked, his red tail wearing a puzzled expression.

"Young redbits are afraid the sun will never return," the Tall One said sadly and seriously. Rensal felt better. The Tall One's words made sense. He kept repeating them to himself as he ran home, redly, through the darkness.

Rensal fell into bed almost before reaching home. He was so tired, his red hair had lost a little lustre and his eyes had bags under them that seemed full of all the worries of his long day. He fell asleep and dreamed about yellow tiger lilies that were chasing red sunflowers up and down the ladder of the sky. He awoke suddenly, leaped out of his dream, and ran and ran between what seemed like columns of tiger lilies and bleeding sunflowers. He did not catch a breath until he reached the Tall One.

"Your words only helped for a while!" Rensal shouted. "When I fell asleep I was afraid all over again."

The Tall One scratched his chin, waiting for a wise expression to appear on his face, and then he said apologetically, "I should have told you about dreams. They are tall tales of wonder and worry that the mind spins out of the leftover wishes of the day when eyes have shut out the images of moonlight and starlight, and look for pictures within." Rensal did not understand these words, but he could hear the kindness in the Tall One's voice and he felt less scared.

He returned home and, if he had more dreams, he did not remember them by the time he awoke in the morning. Before

long, he was outdoors, painting red somersaults in the moist air above the grass. The sun was mopping up the last traces of dew from the earth when Rensal came upon the fallen bird in the stream.

Rensal looked at himself in the mirror of the water and then back at the bird. Rensal put his hands on his shoulders, measuring the size of himself, comparing the feel of his body with what he saw in the water. He was still the same size as yesterday. He had seen fallen birds in the stream before. He knew they were dead but he would never say that word out loud to himself. It was as if his mind were two separate pieces and one piece might scare the other piece away if that word were voiced aloud. The fallen bird was a redwing, and the thought of anything red dying made Rensal shiver. He ran faster than ever like a red wind parting the blades of grass until he reached the Tall One.

"I saw a redwing in the stream. Dead." There. He was brave. He had said the word for the first time and not just to himself but to the Tall One.

The Tall One scratched his chin, but did not wait for a serious expression to enter his face. He had grown very fond of this curious young redbit. When he spoke, there was respect in his voice.

"I am glad you said the word for yourself. It is so hard to explain to someone who has not let himself hear the sound of it for the first time. Death for the redwing and for all of us comes when our eyes are too old to fling the sun back into the sky on that last long-lasting night."

Rensal knew that his words had made the Tall One sad, and it was he who broke the silence first.

"I am small and you are big. You have taught me about shadows, dreams, night, and imagination. Between us, we have four good eyes to light the sun with for many mornings. My red somersaults dance like flowers above the grass and your voice is wise and warm above me like a sheltering roof."

"You are right," said the Tall One. "The world is waiting eagerly for our laughter and our dreams. Let us go at once and pluck the purple nettles in the valley and make some tea."

Rensal began to visit the Tall One practically every day. It became a habit. Yes, Rensal knew what a habit was: he couldn't stop biting his nails at times, no matter how often he was told not to. A habit made a redbit special. Flowers were beautiful, but Rensal never saw a flower with its own habits. Redbits, on the other hand, had peculiar habits that made each one a little different from the other.

Most flowers lean on the wind in the same way. Redbits, on the other hand, play with the wind in a variety of ways. No two redbit somersaults look the same. No two redbits laugh or cry or smile or run or even think the same. Yes, Rensal knew about habits all right, and talking to the Tall One was a habit that was growing on him day by day.

Their first conversation about imagination, dreams, night, and death had whetted Rensal's appetite. To be sure, he was a little scared of the Tall One's candor and did not always understand the meaning of his words, but Rensal was a curious redbit, and he felt he could ask the Tall One almost anything.

This tall one was strangely different from most tall ones: he listened. Your words went into him. When he spoke, his words had rubbed shoulders with yours in his mind. What returned to your ears was a little of yourself, changed by contact with him, and a little of himself, changed by contact with you. It was a game, a wonderful game, and Rensal loved it. The Tall One called it conversation. Rensal had no word for it yet, but he loved it very much all the same.

One day, while gathering the purple nettles for making tea, Rensal surprised the Tall One with a simple question: "Who was your first friend?"

Rensal could practically see the wheels of the Tall One's mind turning backwards to retrieve the memories. Finally, the wheels stopped and the Tall One asked, "Including or excluding parents?" Rensal did not understand the long words beginning with "in" and "ex". So the Tall One made it clear: "Do you want me to count parents in or out?"

"That depends on whether your parents were friendly or not!" Rensal replied rather mischievously. "Were they?" he then asked, with no less mischief in his tone.

"Aha, Rensal, you're something else," laughed the Tall One. Rensal could not imagine what the Tall One meant by "you're something else," but there was no time to interrupt him anyway, as he repeated: "Aha, Rensal, you're something else. You keep me young and on my toes with all your questions. Who was my first friend? Were my parents friendly? Well, I never," and he began to laugh and did not stop until he noticed Rensal was getting offended.

The Tall One wiped the tears of laughter from his eyes and suddenly became serious. "At first, my parents were too tall to be my friends. I loved them and they loved me but we didn't become friends for years, now that I come to think of it. My first friend was, therefore, not one of my parents, but someone else," and he began to scratch his head as if the someone else were hiding under the hair of his scalp. At least, that's how it appeared to Rensal, who always thought that what you did and what you said were connected to each other.

"Your question has really got me going," said the Tall One in amazement. "Where do they come from, such questions? How do you think them up?"

"Well, said Rensal, "this morning I was saying to myself that Ludik was my first friend, when I began to think of Fair-Fair and I wondered if he would be offended that I put Ludik first."

"Who's Fair-Fair?" asked the Tall One.

"Fair-Fair is a satin doll I have owned for as long as I can remember. His real name is Zephyr but I couldn't say that at first. I said Fair-Fair instead and that's what I call him to this day. If I worry about his being offended, does that make him a friend, even if he's not alive?"

"You certainly have a point," conceded the Tall One, and then he began to chuckle. "There I was, wondering if parents were included or excluded and there you were, wondering if Fair-Fairs were included or excluded. What a pair we are!"

Rensal was happy and proud to be called a pair (whatever that was) by the Tall One, which is surely what made him say, "Maybe it's not the first friend in your memory that's so important but the friend you're with at this very moment."

The Tall One blushed a little and poured some some purple nettle tea into a pair of cups.

III

One day, when the Tall One was stoking the coals to heat the water for tea, Rensal said, "Fire and water seem alike to me."

"How so?" asked the Tall One, as the flames began to dance above the rake.

"They flow. They change shape. They are not solid like you and I," said Rensal.

"Yet, we do have fire and water inside us," said the Tall One.

Rensal began to touch himself as if he might reach inside and feel the fire. Finally, in disbelief, he chided the Tall One. "You can't fool me. The water inside us I can understand, but fire—you can't be serious."

The Tall One smiled. "It is difficult to picture fire inside us," he agreed, "but how else could we walk, run, talk, or somersault without a fire inside us to move the muscles, to lift the bones, to turn the wheels so to speak."

Rensal had learnt that whenever the Tall One said "so to speak," he was trying to make something difficult a little easier to understand. So Rensal thought for a minute about the wheels inside him and the fires that turned them.

Rensal always thought of himself as solid through and through. The Tall One was making him think of himself in a

new way. Rensal was not sure he wanted to learn about fires inside him from a tall one who had obviously taken leave of his senses. The Tall One was mad. That explained it. However, the Tall One did not sound mad as he continued.

"Rensal, everything that's alive and can move must build a fire to keep moving. You can't move without energy. Energy is just another name for fire. Even a flower has a hidden fire inside it that helps it to grow and stand up straight in the wind. The flower sucks up food from the earth with its roots and burns it up with air from the sky, and light from the sun to keep itself warm inside out."

Rensal had an immediate picture in his mind of flowers with flames running from root to stem to petal and he began to laugh. He stopped laughing when he began to picture himself as a flower with a mouth instead of roots, lungs bellowing air in and out, and light from the sun entering through his pores into the darkness inside him to kindle the inner fires that moved his muscles.

It was a sober Rensal who finally broke the silence. "Fire and water seem alike to me," he insisted. "They flow. They change shape. They are not solid like you and me."

The Tall One placed his hand on Rensal's shoulder understandingly and asked him if he would like to freshen his tea.

IV

One day, Rensal woke from a dream that troubled him and he could hardly wait to tell the Tall One. In the dream, God was laughing up his sleeve at the redbits who believed in him. Rensal awoke with a sick feeling. God's laughter seemed so evil and the sleeve was the kind of sleeve that could only appear in a dream, a sinister sleeve to say the least. And the poor redbits in the dream seemed so betrayed …

Rensal was in a hurry to reach the Tall One and only washed about half the sleep from himself in his haste. He also knew that dreams had a way of finding perfect hiding places as the day went by. In the morning, he could catch a dream and hold on to it for a while. By afternoon, he couldn't be sure, so Rensal made an early start.

The air seemed young and fresh and not at all drowsy. The sun was beginning to climb the ladder of the sky, but the warmth of it still seemed far off. Rensal ran. The dew drenched his paws as he kicked his way through the grass. The Tall One was lighting his first pipe of the day when Rensal arrived, slightly out of breath from his running. The smoke framed their conversation with an envelope of scented currents as the dialogue began.

"Do you think God would laugh up his sleeve at redbits who believe in him?" Rensal asked, jumping right into the middle of his concerns.

"Such a God would not deserve the attention of redbits," answered the Tall One. He puffed his pipe a few times before he spoke again. "Why do you ask?" he finally said, an emphasis of curiosity on his words.

Rensal told the Tall One his dream, not concealing any of his emotions. The Tall One could see how upset the little one was and he spoke with the gentleness of breezes that pass over leaves without waking them.

"God is a piece of ourselves blown out of proportion. When we lean too heavily on any piece, it may resent the extra weight and before you know it, it turns on us in our dreams as if it were no longer part of us but a stranger."

Rensal heard the words, but the meaning passed right over his head.

"God is a part of ourselves that acts like a stranger?" Rensal asked in disbelief.

"Only sometimes," the Tall One corrected him. "Only sometimes." He chewed on his pipe a little before speaking again. "Most of the time, God is no stranger to us. He is as familiar as sunrise and the gossip of morning birds or streams tinkling in the forest, waiting for ears to discover their hidden bells. God is the familiar feel of your own hand under your chin holding up a hundred heavy thoughts. God is the empty space under blossoms reserved for apples. God is the friendship that has grown between you and me."

Rensal smiled. The Tall One's words seemed to hang in the air above Rensal's head beyond his reach. God as a piece of himself seemed harder to grasp than the fire inside the flower but Rensal understood the part about apples and friendship. If God was nearly always apples and friendship, Rensal could forgive him for occasionally laughing up his sleeve.

The Tall One knew that a few of his words had reached Rensal and he was satisfied. "God is also what gives such special taste to our tea," he said proudly as he poured the steaming liquid into the china cups.

V

At night, Rensal often looked at the sky for hours on end. Sometimes, on very sleepless nights, he even saw the stars disappear into the morning mists. He imagined they were still there hiding in the dawn light. "Most things hide in the dark," Rensal thought to himself, "except stars. They hide in the light."

Rensal thought the moon was the most beautiful star of all, but the others winked at him so much he could hardly give them any less attention. In fact, he played more with the stars than with the moon. The moon had its own name after all and seemed to move around the sky with a mind of its own. The nameless stars were invitations to imagine whatever you fancied.

At night, his wishes hung in the sky, dangling from the stars like candle-lit gifts on a magical tree. Rensal had his own names for the stars, homemade names that made the night as familiar as his own backyard: Runaway, Comeback, Teardrop, Laughing-Eyes, Milk-Spill—these were some of his names for them. Others, he named in clusters according to their shapes: Four-Eyes, Silver-Spade, Night-Spire, Spider-Light, Looking-Glass.

Sometimes, Rensal drew imaginary lines between the stars. It was a favorite night-game. The sky was a ceiling full of animals or faces or luminous rectangles, depending on where you drew the lines. Rensal often fell asleep under a sky full of shimmering animals leaping over fences while drowsy rectangles yawned in the corners of the night.

One evening, when Rensal was thinking up new names for a handful of stars, a new idea streaked across the screen of his mind like a falling meteor. What if the stars were not small specks of light, but huge continents that were so far away they seemed smaller than redbits.

The idea hit Rensal like a sudden thunderclap. At first, he was astonished, then intrigued. He would have run to the Tall One right away if it were morning. He felt the reins of night holding him back and all the horses inside him rearing to go. But he waited and morning eventually climbed over the eastern hills and spilled into the valleys like oceans of color.

The Tall One was taking his morning walk near Stepping Stone Stream, when Rensal tugged at his elbow and tested out his new idea, even before they had time to greet one another.

"Good morning, Rensal," said the Tall One eventually, having waited patiently to get a word in edgewise. This point of etiquette was not lost on the little redbit.

"I'm sorry," apologized Rensal. "I was so full of my own ideas I forgot to say hello, good morning, did you sleep well, or any of our usual greetings. Will you forgive me?"

"Yes of course. And I'll even answer the questions you forgot to ask. I slept very well indeed on my collection of bird feathers, and the morning is especially good, isn't it? Now, let's give your exciting idea the attention it deserves."

Rensal described his night-games to the Tall One. The imaginary strings he tied between the stars, his special names for them, everything. Then he put his new idea into words again. "What if the stars are not scattered pearls, but huge continents of light that seem small only because they are so far away? Mountains look small in the distance, why not stars?"

The Tall One was impressed. He puffed his pipe and sent a billow of smoke skyward. "The smoke that rises up into the sun will have to return one day and tell us if you're right, Rensal."

"Or the birds," said Rensal, wondering how high they reached. "They could tell if they could talk."

"Their songs are apparently enough for them," said the Tall One. "They have no need of our long-winded ways of speaking."

"If we had their wings, we wouldn't just sing. We'd leap into the sky and pull down the stars and …"

"And then you couldn't tie them up in strings at night to amuse yourself when you're lonely," the Tall One reminded him humorously.

"There would be no more night if I had wings," said Rensal defiantly. "I'd not only pull down the stars, I'd follow the sun."

"You'd get very tired. You'd miss the night after a while," said the Tall One wisely.

"Oh," said Rensal in disgust. "I hate your wisdom sometimes. It clips my wings."

"I am sorry, Rensal. Perhaps I am becoming an old grey-haired spoilsport. Your ideas are beautiful and your imagination has a thousand wings. Who knows?" said the Tall One expansively. "Maybe one day, redbits will fling their nets into the sky and bring home a catch the whole world will never stop talking about."

Rensal felt refueled by the Tall One's words, and his mind began to race again. "Do you suppose there could be other redbits living out there in the continents? I mean, in the stars?" asked the wide-eyed little one.

"If there are," said the Tall One, chuckling, "I hope they've discovered friendship, purple nettles, and the taste of tea."

They both laughed, looking up at the sky with four miraculous eyes.

VI

One day, Rensal was playing with Ludik and Silitar. They were running to and fro in the grass, like flames parting and becoming one again. The wind ran in and out between them, like a fourth player, eager to join in. Their voices rose and fell, accompanying their games like music. The sun, from afar, added heat to their rhythms. Stepping Stone Stream blew a breeze from its throat to cool them. In the small

world of their play, they seemed as far from the commerce of the Tall World as night from day. But not for long.

They had played "Acorns," "Hear a Leaf," and were in the middle of "Touch the Sky," when Rensal brought everything to a halt with one of his questions. This habit of Rensal's, needless to say, did not endear him to his friends. A game was something to be played, not questioned. In fact, there was nothing like questions for destroying the rhythm of a good game.

"Acorns" was a game redbits loved to play. When redbits were being called home from the fields for bedtime, nine times out of ten you can be sure Acorns was the game that was being interrupted. Acorns was so simple, yet so enjoyable. "How many acorns in my fist? How many acorns on your list?" one redbit would shout with his fist raised and the others would have to guess. The correct guess brought possession of another fistful of acorns. A good guesser could amass a small fortune of acorns by nightfall. There were bad guessers, of course, and fists were often raised for reasons other than counting. But the rhythms of games have their own ways of re-establishing order, as you know.

"Hear a Leaf" was also a very popular game. One redbit would sneak over a blanket of dry leaves as silently as possible. The others, with their backs turned would shout, "I hear a leaf," whenever the least crackle of leaves gave the intruder away. Some redbits were such silent scouts their paws seemed weightless even on the driest leaves. Some redbits could hear leaves crackling before paws touched them. This could lead to arguments, but, as I say, games have an order that usually prevails.

It was in the middle of "Touch the Sky," you will remember, that Rensal ruined everything with a question. "Touch the Sky" is another favorite of redbits, making Rensal's question even more unwelcome.

Redbits are nimble tree-climbers. They are small and although they weigh more than leaves, at the end of the slenderest branches, pretending to touch the sky, they seem to defy gravity. They are not weightless, of course, and eventually their skyward excursions on thread-like branches bring them down to earth, but not before they've shouted, "I touched the sky!" The sky is touched by many redbit paws, as you can imagine. Each one claiming priority as the game proceeds, until the sky eventually withdraws from redbits and returns to the stars.

"Where do games come from?" was the question Rensal asked in the middle of Touch the Sky that brought all activity to a standstill.

"Oh, shush," cried the others. "You and your questions! Just play the game."

Rensal felt stupid that he had asked and he returned to the game, but his curiosity did not leave and he vowed to put the question to the Tall One as soon as the opportunity arose.

Next morning, Rensal did not join Ludik and Silitar for their usual games. Instead, he made his way eagerly towards the Tall One, following Stepping Stone Stream to the tunnel of leaves, which got its name from the willows on both sides joining branches above the stream to form an arch.

On hot summer days this tunnel was the shadiest and coolest place for miles, and many redbits envied the Tall One for living so close to it. The Tall One would sit for hours bathing his feet in the stream, the smoke from his pipe climbing lazily towards the arch of leaves. In fact, it was here that Rensal found him, staring into the stream as if he could see things in there that no one else could.

"What's in there?" Rensal asked.

"My own thoughts," said the Tall One immediately, as if he had expected the question or was perhaps answering his own silent question that Rensal put words to. Suddenly, they both realized they were in the middle of conversation without a greeting between them.

"Good morning, Rensal," said the Tall One. "We started in the middle again, didn't we? We're getting to know each other so well. Like a pair of shoes you're so familiar with they become like a part of yourself. You don't have to put them on. They slip on by themselves." The Tall One chuckled and Rensal smiled. He wasn't very old yet but he knew shoes like that and he knew what the Tall One meant.

"Good morning," said Rensal. "We were in the middle, and I didn't even ask the question I came prepared with. In fact, I think I've forgotten it."

"It will come back if you give it half a chance," said the Tall One with a wise expression on his face. "In fact, I know a game called Lost and Found that brings forgotten things back into your mind."

"That's it!" said Rensal.

"My oh my, I've never seen it work that fast before," said the Tall One in amazement.

"No, No," said Rensal, explaining. "When you said game, I remembered immediately what I wanted to ask you. Where do games come from? That's my question. When I asked Ludik and Silitar, they shouted me down. My curiosity ruins things at times," Rensal added sadly.

"I know what you mean," said the Tall One, with such an expression on his face that Rensal felt completely understood. "But I would never relinquish curiosity for popularity, Rensal, even if it gets you into trouble at times. Even if it gets you into trouble at times," he repeated, and his voice trailed off into a private silent place that even Rensal could not enter. In a moment, however, he was back to the conversation enthusiastically.

"Where do games come from? What a magnificent question! Even if we never discover the answer, what a peach of a question," said the Tall One loudly and expressively, lifting his feet out of the stream and walking up and down excitedly, as if he had discovered one of the wonders of the world.

This was one of the things about the Tall One that Rensal loved most. The question was more fun than the answer for him it seemed, and to think of peaches and questions in the same breath, what a funny way of thinking the Tall One had. And yet Rensal's head was full of peaches as he watched the Tall One playing with the question the way a cat experiments with a spool of thread.

"Where do games come from?" the Tall One finally repeated in a more serious, reflective tone. "We can't ask tall ones," he continued, like a lawyer sifting the sources of evidence. "They've forgotten all their games. We can't ask young redbits. They'll say, 'shush, you're spoiling our games with your questions.' What a delicious dilemma," said the Tall One as he began to march up and down, shaking his head, scratching his temple, and chuckling to himself, like the mad redbits Rensal had read about, who get that way after eating the berries that make you see things that are not really there at all. Rensal did not know what "dilemma" meant but "delicious" made him think of peaches all over again.

"Are there any books we can look it up in?" asked Rensal, trying to be helpful.

"It's not the kind of thing people write about," said the Tall One sadly. "Books are full of the history of love and hatred, arts and sciences, but important subjects like games never get written about. Or if they do, the books gather dust on library shelves: never opened by redbit paws, the pages never seen by redbit eyes, the words never heard by redbit ears. Forgive me, Rensal. There I go again, sounding like an old spoilsport cynic. You are right to think of consulting books. Maybe there are books on the topic of redbit games. And if there are none, I swear by this tunnel of leaves you and I shall write them," said the Tall One triumphantly.

"I can make a list of all the games I know," said Rensal, the enthusiasm spreading from tall one to little one with the speed of fire.

"And I can try to dredge my memory for all the forgotten games of my young days," said the Tall One, his eyes beginning to look within.

"What about the game of Lost & Found that you told me about? Would that help? How do you play that game anyway?" Rensal asked, the three questions tumbling out in one breath.

"The game works for recently forgotten things. I don't know if it would work for long-ago forgotten things," said the Tall One doubtfully.

"How do you find the recently forgotten items?" asked Rensal, eager to learn a new trick.

"Simple," said the Tall One. "You just try to remember whatever's forgotten, saying all the wrong words that come to mind. Eventually, the wrong words lead you back like a trail of stepping stones to the forgotten word." The Tall One spoke with such conviction about the game that Rensal never doubted it would work. In fact, he couldn't wait to try it the next time his memory played a trick on him.

"It will be like getting even with memory, playing a trick back on it," thought Rensal, and the idea pleased him so much he began to chuckle to himself. Then he asked the Tall One why it wouldn't work on memories forgotten long ago.

"That's a lot of stepping stones back to the old days, Rensal," said the Tall One with a faraway look in his eyes, as if the distance he was trying to grasp was way out of reach. "A lot of stepping stones," he said again, half to himself, half to Rensal, as if he was weary already from the length of the journey.

"I'll carry your bags," said Rensal humorously.

"I know you will," said the Tall One, encouraged by the little one's confidence. "And let us bathe our feet in the stream for a while, before we begin our journey," said the Tall One

with a wink that added another level to Rensal's humor. They both laughed, the sounds flowing into each other like currents in a stream.

"This stream could tell us a few things, throw us a few clues if only it could talk," said the Tall One after a pause.

"Do you suppose it could tell us who the first redbits were and why they invented games?" asked Rensal excitedly, his imagination beginning to pick up speed. "Suppose the first redbit played with his paws, hiding them behind his back pretending to look for them, and discovering them, joyfully, only after the most exhaustive of searches. Suppose he told his game to a friend and so on, and so on, from the beginning of time to forever after. Suppose all the tall ones forgot the games, and suppose the games of little redbits were the only surviving links in the chain of memory."

Rensal was wide-eyed, as if he could see from one end of the world to the other. The first redbits and the last, their paws behind their backs, and the whole history of redbit games slung between them like an endless string.

"Suppose and pretend are such beautiful words. I hope you never stop using them," said the Tall One admiringly.

"Do you suppose we can follow the string, back to the first redbits and their games?" asked Rensal hopefully.

"With words like 'suppose' and 'pretend' to guide us, we have a head start and there's no knowing where it might lead to," said the Tall One genuinely.

As they left the tunnel of leaves, they could both almost see the invisible string that was pulling them and guiding them all at once.

VII

When anyone asked Rensal what he would wish to be if he couldn't be a redbit, without hesitation he always gave the same answer: "A bird."

At first, Rensal loved birds because they had wings but gradually he began to love their singing even more than their flight. It was birdsong that rinsed his face with music in the mornings, pulling him out of darkness into the light of day.

If Rensal had his way, birdsong would accompany him everywhere, as intimate and constant as his own shadow. Rensal could imitate their music and when the birds deserted him, he conjured them up again with the magic of mimicry. It was quite a sight and quite a sound to discover Rensal in rehearsal, but this was rare since he liked to keep his artistry a secret from everyone. But not from the Tall One.

The Tall One would probably never have known of Rensal's musical interest, had the topic of secrets not cropped up one day in conversation.

"Flowers have no secrets. They wear everything on their sleeves," the Tall One was explaining. "Only redbits have secrets. In fact, secrets make redbits unique." The Tall One's way of turning what seemed like vices into virtues always astonished Rensal. A secret, in the Tall One's opinion, was the mind's magic, nothing to be ashamed of.

"The mind has many hiding places. Secrets are the ones we know about," the Tall One added mysteriously. It was then that Rensal decided to share his secret with him, beginning hesitantly but gradually slipping into total trust.

"I, ah, have a secret. I, ah, imitate birds. I know they wake everyone in the morning. But I take it personally as if they were singing only to me. And when I can't hear them and I miss them, I fill in for myself with my own home-made music." Rensal demonstrated his talent, blowing the notes confidently through the small aperture of his lips and sounding for all the world like a loquacious redwing.

"That's incredible," said the Tall One. "If I hadn't heard it with my own ears, I would have sworn it was a redwing and not an imitation."

Rensal was embarrassed by the praise and would not speak for many minutes. The Tall One filled the silence with his musings. "I suppose we got the idea of music from the birds. But where did they get it from, eh, Rensal?" Rensal thought for a while. The Tall One's question dropped like a pebble into his mind. You could almost see the ripples.

"Music is playing with sound. If we could discover who made the first sounds we'd have the answer, wouldn't we?"

"Not quite," said the Tall One. "Making sounds and playing with them is not quite the same thing, is it now, Rensal?" Rensal knew that he would have to agree with the Tall One, who was continuing to make his point. "You see, Rensal, a stream can make sounds but we wouldn't call it music, would we?"

"Maybe the birds heard the streams and began to imitate them," cried Rensal excitedly. "That could be music, couldn't it?"

"Yes," said the Tall One, "and they need not have confined themselves to streams. The wind sounds like an orchestra at

times, doesn't it, as it whispers or screams on the back of the weather?"

"What about muttering rain?" asked Rensal.

"Or crickets playing with their legs in the night?" said the Tall One.

"Or fire crackling as the flames dance?," said Rensal.

"Or thunder like a distant drum?" said the Tall One.

"Or the songs of whinnying horses?" said Rensal.

"Or the rustle of leaves?" said the Tall One.

"Or the sea breathing in and out?" said Rensal.

"Or redbit laughter?" suggested the Tall One. At this, they both began to chuckle, their voices like two instruments taking time from each other. Finally they stopped laughing, and the Tall One said, "Yes, I guess the birds had their choice of sounds to imitate. But how did they find such beautiful trails in all those forests of sound, Rensal?"

"Perhaps we'll never know," said Rensal mischievously. "Maybe it's a secret!"

The Tall One gave Rensal a knowing look and began to laugh again, the notes spilling out of him like the most liquid music.

VIII

After a conversation with the Tall One, Rensal would often continue the dialogue with himself. He would think of things he wished he had said, reminding himself to bring them up next time.

At such moments, Rensal seemed out of contact with the world around him, and was often called absent-minded by his friends. But it was not absent at all: In fact his mind was a canvas full of trial colors where words and images reviewed the scenes of the past and tried to peek into the future.

For instance, in their last conversation they had spoken about music and Rensal, in retrospect, could not for the life of him understand how poetry had stayed out of the reckoning. He wrote poetry. In secret, to be sure, but there were fewer and fewer secrets between him and the Tall One, so that could hardly explain his omission. "Next time," Rensal said to himself, bringing the internal monologue to a close.

Next time, not surprisingly, turned out to be the following morning. It was the kind of morning that could pull poetry from stones, if you know what I mean. The sky was a sheet of white and blue, mixed so delicately it was impossible to say where one began and the other left off. The earth was moist and gently reaching for the sun. The stream was beginning to play with the fringes of light. The music of the birds was stitching the many fabrics of the world into one seamless piece of cloth.

Rensal walked beside the water. Every breath was a magic potion, an inspiration of joy. Before long, he was playing with a phrase, the way a fisherman handles a trout.

"The sky is in the stream like a face in a mirror or the shape of a dream in the mind of a river."

Rensal wasn't sure if it made sense but the sound appealed to him. He didn't want to sacrifice all reason for rhyme's sake but a poem without music in it made no sense to him at all.

"The sky is riding on the prancing stream
Like a sleeper, bareback on the shoulders of a dream."

He liked the second effort better than the first. He would discuss it with the Tall One. It would be fun. Suddenly, he found himself wondering if the Tall One wrote poetry. The idea amused him. They would have something new to talk about.

When Rensal reached the Tall One's house beyond the bend in Stepping Stone Stream, the water for tea was steaming above the fire and the pipe smoke rushed to greet him like an old friend.

"Good morning, Rensal," said the Tall One. "Perfect timing. The kettle is singing, the bread is toasting, the pipe is puffing, the earth is turning, and you and I are talking. What more could we ask for?"

"Poetry," said Rensal nonchalantly, yet aware that he was jumping right into the middle of things.

"Poetry!" said the Tall One, surprised by the suddenness of the topic.

"Sorry," said Rensal. "Let me explain." And he told the Tall One how their dialogue about music had in turn become a monologue about poetry.

"Poetry is second only to music in redbit attempts to be divine," said the Tall One grandly. "As gods, surely we would have music while awake and poetry whilst asleep."

Naturally, this speech encouraged Rensal and he promptly tested out both versions of the poem on the Tall One.

"For some reason I like the second version better also," said the Tall One, after a pause like a wine taster who has given the mouth enough time to weigh a difference in taste.

"I see you like rhyme," said the Tall One later, after toast and tea. He puffed on his pipe a few times and continued.

"When I was your age I loved rhyme, too. I couldn't resist the sing-song lilt of it! To tell you the truth, the words were mere vehicles for the rhyme." He puffed again thoughtfully before continuing.

"Forgive me, Rensal. Am I sounding like an old spoilsport again? What are we old redbits to do? Memory is a terrible wedge between us and young ones. No wonder old age is a monument that young pigeons defile!"

"I'm surprised at you," said Rensal indignantly. "You are not a monument and I am not a pigeon. I came here to talk seriously about poetry."

The Tall One was taken aback. Rensal's lack of sentimentality was unexpected and refreshing. An awkward silence eventually pulled words from both of them slowly, and the damp kindling of conversation suddenly caught fire again.

"What have you got against rhyme?" Rensal asked somewhat offensively.

"I've nothing against it! I just think rhyme is everywhere in poetry and need not be confined to the end of the line. Every word has the potential of rhyme in a poem. Every word is ready to burst into song!

"Give an example," Rensal said provocatively.

The Tall One was caught off-guard for an instant but recovered quickly and began to recite in slow melodious tones:

"Time-Out
Sky opens,
Rain falls,
Wind puts a frown
On the river.
Fish go deeper,
Redbits shelter,
Play suspended.
Sky opens,
Rain falls,

38

Redbits go deeper
To remember."

"I like it," said Rensal genuinely. "I can just see the fish going deeper!"

"Do you miss the rhyme?" asked the Tall One expectantly.

"Yes," replied Rensal honestly. "But it has a rhythm. It sings even without the rhyme. How did you do it?"

"I cannot imitate birdsong like you, Rensal. I had to try to learn to sing with words," said the Tall One.

"Poems are songs without music, you mean?" asked Rensal.

"That's a nice way of putting it," mused the Tall One, reciting his poem again. The sounds of his song without music gently stirring the currents of air.

IX

Rensal, though young, was becoming aware that life was not all play, nor all music and poetry either. There was fear and illness and death also, dark shadows that jostled with light for space.

War was another word that had recently entered his vocabulary. "The war is over," he heard one tall one say expressively to another.

Rensal had not known that the war was on, or what war was for that matter, but it did seem to be something that was better over, that you're better off without. He wondered if it was a subject he could discuss with the Tall One. He would find a way to ease it into the conversation.

Next morning, on his way to the Tall One's, he picked some berries from the bushes beside the stream. "They will go well with toast and tea," he thought to himself. The berries hid their dark rich colors under leaves and thorns, but Rensal's fingers could have plucked them in darkness without missing one or pricking himself. When his basket was full of berries beyond the brim, he hurried past the bend in the stream towards his destination.

The Tall One was chasing the squirrels out of his cabbage patch when Rensal arrived. "Those scurrilous squirmy

squirrels," the Tall One was screaming, searching for the fiercest words and throwing his slippers with the accuracy of a blind man. Rensal thought it a good time to try out his new word. "You are at war with them," Rensal cried tentatively.

"You bet I'm at war with them. It's unending. I chase them. They return. But I will preserve my cabbages from them if it takes a fight to the finish." The Tall One was fuming, as if there was more at stake than cabbages. Rensal was convinced he had used the word properly, even if he did not know what it meant. When things calmed down, Rensal explained his discovery of the word and his trial use of it.

"I'm sorry I gave you the first opportunity to use the word," said the Tall One apologetically. "Forgive me, Rensal. It's not one of redbits' proudest creations. War, I mean, not words," he added softly.

"If it exists, we might as well have a word for it," said Rensal, trying to be wise.

"I do wish we had no use for the word," said the Tall One sadly.

"Who used the word first?" asked Rensal, who as you will remember, was obsessed with the beginnings of things.

"I think there have always been wars, maybe even before there were words," said the Tall One thoughtfully. "The first redbit to use the word left a tragic legacy to the rest of us," the Tall One continued, his voice trailing off as if the content became too heavy for words to carry.

"The wars must be very far away if I haven't even heard the word up to now," said Rensal consolingly.

"Yes, war does seem far from this valley, far from the stream," said the Tall One, bending down to touch the water the way you pat an animal you love. "But beyond these hills, redbits redden the earth with their own blood as often as the sun rises." Rensal was beginning to understand the word. Its meaning rumbled in his mind like thunder.

"Do they fight over acorns?" he asked innocently, remembering the game and the raised fists.

"They fight over everything," said the Tall One sadly. "Acorns and anthills, music and memory, valleys and streams." Rensal could understand fighting over acorns; the rest of it puzzled him but he didn't dare ask for explanations. He knew a tender topic when he stumbled on it.

"Will it ever end? Will it ever be different?" asked Rensal hopefully.

"Once blood is spilt, Rensal, you can't pour it back again," said the Tall One, "and redbits have a way of remembering blood that was spilt even longer than blood that wasn't." This sounded strange to Rensal, but again he did not question it. He merely said under his breath, "Redbits would be better off without any blood in that case."

"What did you say?" asked the Tall One quietly, his voice still weary with the burden of his previous thoughts.

"Redbits would be better off without blood in that case," said Rensal, raising his voice.

"Oh, no," said the Tall One, recovering his usual enthusiasm. "Remember the fire I told you about that each redbit must build to keep the wheels turning? It's blood that carries the wind from lungs to food to build the fires in the depths of the body. We couldn't survive for long without it," said the Tall One seriously. "There would be no laughter without blood," continued the Tall One convincingly.

"And no tears either," said Rensal, stubbornly, still thinking of wars.

"Rensal, Rensal, some words are harder to understand than others. I have been under the sun and under the moon for many days and nights longer than you, thinking about this new word you learned only today, and I still don't understand it. I understand my little wars with myself and with the squirrels. The rest I leave for redbits wiser than myself to struggle with." The Tall One seemed defeated by his own thoughts and it was Rensal who broke the silence.

"I am sorry I picked up this new word. I should have confined my pickings to berries."

They both laughed. After all, the tea was mellow, the berries shone on the toast like rubies, and the wars were hidden beyond the stream, beyond the valley, behind the hills and far away.

X

One evening, Rensal fell asleep in the meadow under a quilt of stars and dreamt a dream that ruined the beauty of the night with its sinister plot.

In the morning, the dream made off in a hurry like darkness running from the dawn light but Rensal closed his eyes, strained hard, and held on to the vanishing images for dear life. His tenacity was rewarded and soon he had all the images on a string in his mind in a shining sequence: In the dream, a redbit looked in a mirror and watched the color fading from his hair, like rubies turning paler than snow in a flash. Without color, he could hardly recognize himself. But there was worse to come. When he met his redbit friends, they teased him and called him names, "Whitebit, whitebit, what an ugly sight-bit," and they laughed and laughed.

In the dream, the laughter felt like a knife of shame that sliced the poor whitebit into several pieces; each piece trying to hide from the other in humiliation.

When Rensal awoke he felt convinced for a moment that he was the whitebit. That moment seemed longer in duration than many a day or night to Rensal until he reached the mirror of the stream and saw a familiar redbit looking back at him in relief. Rensal sighed. He sat down beside the drowsy stream, exhausted already first thing in the morning.

He scratched his head. Where had it come from? Such a dream! Would the Tall One know how such an idea had found a way into his head?

Rensal looked at the stream and into the stream, as if the answers lay folded between its surface and depth. The stream moved beside him quivering with morning light; more like a living thing than a mobile of reflections. "If you could only speak," he mused to himself, not out loud but quietly within, in the silent space where words are born without a sound, far from the wind and the mouth.

"Redbits have a surface and a depth too you know," said Rensal half to himself and half to the stream. "We are just as mysterious as you, even more so. You hold the sun on your

lap and change colors many times to keep up with the sun, but other streams don't tease you for it, and I'll bet you never have a sleepless night."

Rensal turned on his heel and left the stream indignantly, as if it were a real conversation that had ended in a quarrel.

When he reached the Tall One, he was still fighting with the stream and the Tall One sensed it. "Got out on the wrong side of bed this morning, eh, Rensal?" began the Tall One with a mixture of concern and mischief.

"I slept in the meadow," said Rensal abruptly. The silence of the night that lingers quietly in the first folds of the morning filled the space between the two friends like a presence you could touch.

"We should say hello before we fight," the Tall One suggested awkwardly. "And tea might help," he added with more warmth.

"Oh, I'm sorry," said Rensal. "I don't want to fight. I'm still dreaming, I guess, and walking in my sleep."

The Tall One prepared some tea and Rensal told him the dream. "Where could it have come from?" asked Rensal, as if the dream were an intruder, not one of the usual creatures of his imagination.

"Prejudice," said the Tall One, the word falling from his mouth in three pieces. The first syllable like the weight of an axe being raised slowly, the two final syllables falling swiftly like the rush of the downswing. The word hit Rensal like steel.

"What is it?" asked Rensal. "I don't like the sound of it. What does it mean?"

The Tall One chewed on his pipe, a little as if he were thinking with his mouth. "It's hating yourself and taking it out on an innocent bystander," said the Tall One, weighing his words as if there were a scale at hand. Rensal didn't understand but he thought immediately of the stream and how harshly he had spoken to it. "It's pinning the blame before the crime is even committed," the Tall One continued.

"But why?" said Rensal. And he repeated it many times. "But why?"

The Tall One walked up and down, his face a collage of expressions like sunlight on the stream shifting from side to side. Rensal saw fear and doubt and curiosity and other emotions moving between surface and depth on the Tall One's face. "It's easier to throw a stone at someone else than at yourself," said the Tall One.

"But I was throwing stones at myself in the dream," said Rensal wisely. "I was the whitebit and I invented my own bad dream."

The Tall One was impressed. "Yes, indeed," he said, "you threw the stone at yourself in your sleep. But why?"

"I asked you first," said Rensal playfully. They both laughed.

"Prejudice," said Rensal after a pause, testing out the new word cautiously like a redbit placing less than all his weight on a slender branch in a game of Touch the Sky. "It is a sinister word," he thought as this strange new word led him slowly backwards towards the evil in his dream.

"White means losing red," Rensal said finally. "Yesterday I lost many acorns playing with Ludik and Silitar. The dream was a variation of that, except that I lost more than a fistful of playthings. I practically lost myself."

The Tall One was proud of Rensal's excursions into the territory of his dreams. "You have returned from the kingdom of sleep with a piece of the night in your hands and you have made a little sense out of it. Bravo, Rensal!" said the Tall One, waving his pipe like a conductor.

The praise made Rensal's tail flutter. "It was only a dream. I'm no hero," he said modestly, but he could still hear the Tall One's words ringing inside him like applause.

"It was only a dream, to be sure," said the Tall One seriously, "But I have heard that in the land of the five-fingered, people go to war over color and actually spill blood."

"They end up the same color with blood all over them; all redbits in the end," Rensal thought to himself sadly. He looked down at the three digits of his own tiny paws and tried to picture the land of the five-fingered, but he could not. They both seemed lost in their thoughts until humor rescued them.

"We only fight about acorns," said Rensal.

"And cabbage," said the Tall One. They laughed and their faces rippled with the sudden relief of laughter like a couple of babbling streams. Then they indulged a favorite prejudice for nettles, and had some more tea.

XI

One day, after Rensal had seen the redwing in the stream, he wondered what became of it. At first, he was afraid to touch it or even look at it. Later, he couldn't get it out of his mind.

What became of it after it drowned in the stream? Was there a history of redwings, or was there only a history of famous redwings? Were redwings who intimidated the wind with their flight remembered, while redwings who lost their hold of the wind were forgotten? If this was history, one were better off without it, thought Rensal to himself sadly.

"History doesn't exist," said the Tall One, when Rensal arrived with his dilemma. "Redwings exist and the wind exists and death exists and memory exists but history doesn't exist."

"What's the difference, then, between memory and history?" asked Rensal, trying to follow the logic.

"Memory is alive. History is dead," said the Tall One bluntly.

"But isn't history a way to keep the dead alive?" asked Rensal.

"Yes," said the Tall One, "But we can only keep the famous living. The forgotten are dead forever."

"What a peach of a problem," said Rensal. "Let's try to bring the forgotten back to life."

"You'll have to count the seasons and count the fallen leaves and count the hours of sleep you lose with your nonsense of numbers," laughed the Tall One.

"You mean there are not enough numbers to number the forgotten?" asked Rensal sadly.

"Yes," said the Tall One. "We had to use our numbers in a useful way."

"... like how many tea leaves make a good cup of tea, you mean?" asked Rensal.

"No," said the Tall One wisely. "Come on, Rensal, you and I know it only takes two to enjoy the taste of fallen leaves or purple nettles without counting them. The history of leaves is the memory of taste, nothing more or less."

"'More' and 'less' must have been the first numbers," said Rensal, riding on the Tall One's words.

"That's another story," said the Tall One, pouring tea into one cup after the other.

XII

One day, Rensal was counting on his paws—three digits on one paw, three on the other. Suddenly, he said to himself, "If there were no parts of the body to count on, I bet there would be no numbers. Would the Tall One agree with me?" he wondered to himself.

Looking around him, suddenly he could see numbers everywhere: five flowers looking at themselves in the stream; hundreds of leaves above him; one sun; one sky; two white clouds chasing one other; eleven or more redbits in the distance, stirring the landscape a little with their play. "Could it all have begun on my fingers? What a peach of a question," he whispered to himself, mimicking the Tall One.

When Rensal had a question such as this, there was an extra bounce in his legs as he made his way towards the Tall One. The question fluttered inside him like a bird in a cage trying to get out. The Tall One must have sensed Rensal's eagerness, since he greeted him by saying:

"Before you ask the question that is burning a hole in your tongue, would you like some tea? I still have a few of those delicious berries left to crown your toast with."

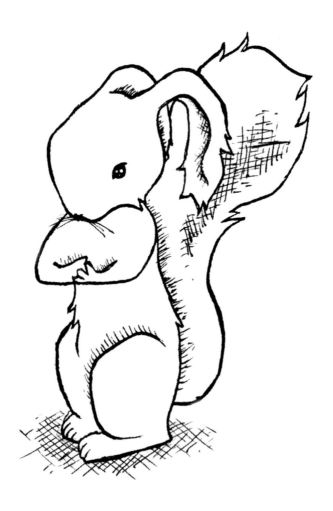

Rensal suddenly had a humorous thought that if war broke out, if volcanos spilt lava into the valley, if the sky fell into Stepping Stone Stream, the Tall One would still be serving toast and tea before discussing the catastrophe. Rensal had trouble dismissing this humorous thought from his mind and answering the Tall One's question.

After a piece of toast, washed down with some well-brewed tea, Rensal did discuss his theory.

"What a peach of a question. Where do you find them?" The Tall One poured some tea and continued thoughtfully, "If you are right, perhaps the first numbers—one and two— refer to the first two talkers: you and me, your body, a pair of bodies, one and two. In fact, I'll bet two came first, if you know what I mean. It took two to discover one."

"Yes," said Rensal excitedly. "Two bodies talking discovered two and then one, and the little parts of the body could be used for the other numbers. I have heard that in the land of the five-fingered, the number six means jump to the other hand. In our land, it would have to be four." said Rensal, his eyes jumping from one three-fingered paw to the other.

"I suppose we count differently then," said the Tall One thoughtfully. "Though I can't imagine the world cares very much how we number it. It will probably still be turning when we have forgotten all our numbers."

"How do you know it turns?" asked Rensal doubtfully.

"The moon moves. I always imagine that we move too, just to keep up with her, Rensal," laughed the Tall One. The Tall One lit his morning pipe and continued, "We couldn't number the stars without redbit fingers. Imagine that, Rensal," said the Tall One, stretching himself as if he might touch the sky if he wished to.

"Redbits cannot help putting their paws into everything," said the Tall One, returning to the original topic. "We like to touch, and what we cannot touch, at least we can number."

"The numbers reach beyond us. They are our wings, I suppose," said Rensal, moving his paws like a bird in flight, without realizing it.

"And hopefully not our downfall," said the Tall One, moving his paw through the air like a fallen bird.

"You are still thinking of war," said Rensal.

"Yes," said the Tall One sadly. "We number what we own. Before long we are willing to fight over numbers."

"Like the squirrel and your cabbages," said Rensal teasingly.

"Yes, exactly," said the Tall One, taking him seriously. "I have numbered the cabbage, and I'm willing to fight for it.

"You think we'd be better off without numbers?" asked Rensal.

"Sometimes I wonder," said the Tall One emphatically.

"But suppose they could lead us to the stars," said Rensal, his eyes shining with visions beyond his reach. "Suppose they could lead us to the stars," he repeated.

The Tall One did not answer. Rensal was silent, too, looking back and forth, first at his paws and then the sky, as if both were numbers he could count on. Then he looked at the Tall One and back at his own paws, whispering, "Me and you, one and two."

"Yes, quite a pair," said the Tall One, and this time Rensal knew what the word meant.

XIII

One morning, after toast and a thousand questions, the Tall One said to Rensal quietly, "You have asked me many questions about beginnings, but never have you asked me how redbits begin."

"I only ask you what I don't already know," said Rensal simply.

"You mean you know how redbits are made and given birth to?" asked the Tall One in surprise.

"Yes, I've seen birth in the fields many times," said Rensal matter-of-factly.

"And you know what slender seeds support our origins?" said the Tall One, not sure if he was asking a question or stating a fact.

"Yes, I've seen the animals in the fields. At first, I thought they were fighting. Then I knew it was not war but love. They were sharing pieces of themselves with each other so that new animals could be made out of the old."

"Tall ones creating little ones," added Rensal philosophically, simply, as if the mystery had been solved without difficulty.

"Well," said the Tall One, "You're something else."

"No," said the little one. "I'm still Rensal, even if I have figured these things out. By the way, it was not as easy as it sounds. At first, I believed the tall tales about storks and births under cabbages. Then I began to notice redbits getting fatter and fatter for a few months and then skinny again but carrying a tiny, newborn weight around; a tiny redbit that had not existed before. I put two and two together, if you know what I mean."

"I know what you mean," said the Tall One wisely. He lit another pipe and puffed a few times. "Why is it so hard to discuss?" he asked finally.

"You mean tall ones find it hard to talk about?" said Rensal teasingly.

"Oh, come on, Rensal," said the Tall One. "Why is it so hard to talk about?"

Rensal thought for a while, looking deeply at the flow of the stream. The water filed past, ignorant of his thoughts. "Little ones are afraid to believe there was a time before they arrived. Little redbits are afraid to believe they came from dark spaces inside other redbits. They prefer to imagine they were always here."

"And tall ones?" said the Tall One, inviting Rensal to continue his argument.

"Tall ones like to pretend that little ones know nothing. Telling them things would make the little ones taller in their eyes and the tall ones would like to keep the little ones small forever." Rensal had been moving his paws around to dramatize his points. He now joined them together as if to show that he had finished.

"But don't you think little ones want to keep tall ones tall forever also?" asked the Tall One, trying to reopen the conversation.

Rensal was silent for what seemed like ages before he spoke. "Yes," he finally answered. "Little ones would like to keep tall ones tall forever also." The Tall One looked down at Rensal. The little one looked up. The distance between them had never been smaller.

XIV

One September day, when the air was sharp and the light was brilliant, Rensal watched the autumn leaves falling. He gathered a few and carried them to the Tall One.

"Spring and summer have passed. They have left their shadows behind in these leaves," said Rensal like a poet.

"Even their shadows are beautiful," said the Tall One consolingly.

"I remember my first autumn," said Rensal. "No one had told me about seasons. I thought the trees were on fire."

"Yes," said the Tall One. "Flames falling out of the trees in many shapes and colors, giving a visible form to the invisible wind. I know what you mean."

"I was really afraid the first time," said Rensal honestly.

"But from then on you called it a season and you were no longer afraid," said the Tall One knowingly.

"Yes, the word helped. Everything was falling down, but the word 'season' made sense out of it," said Rensal.

"A word that helpful should be used more than four times a year," laughed the Tall One.

"There are seasons, I suppose, that were never given names," said Rensal.

"How do you mean?" asked the Tall One curiously.

"I mean that the weather wears its heart on its sleeve. Redbits hide their seasons within. They often change without knowing and without putting a name to the change," said Rensal, sounding older than his years.

"Yes," said the Tall One, his voice coming from a very deep place inside him. "Our seasons are many and nameless."

A silence fell between the two like a bridge they were afraid to cross. Finally, Rensal took the first step.

"We do have kinds of seasons as we grow from small to tall," said Rensal, trying to turn a question into a statement.

"On the outside, yes," agreed the Tall One. "Our flesh has the quality of leaves. I believe we shed it all the time and renew it without knowing. But on the inside ..." His voice trailed off, returning to some hidden place within where the first words were born out of the first feelings.

"On the inside, every moment of a redbit's life can be a season once he has seen a fallen redwing in a stream," said Rensal, like a young redbit that has suddenly grown old.

"My, how you've grown," said the Tall One.

"Yes," laughed Rensal. "The seasons are inside me, but in a way I'm older than them."

"And more thoughtful," added the Tall One. "Their leaves fall, but they would never dream of picking some up and making a gift out of them to a tall one."

To Rensal, the Tall One's words were a gift also, seasoned from within, and falling softly like leaves of love.

XV

Having discussed the beginnings of each important thing that had ever entered his mind, one day Rensal had the idea to discuss where his interest in beginnings came from in the first place.

"What a perfect peach of a question," said Rensal to himself, knowing that the Tall One would get as much of a kick out of it as he did. Rensal looked at the stream that kept him company as he walked. Did it care about its beginnings, the first seeds of water in the high rocks close to the sky that gathered speed, trying to make a name for themselves? Were beginnings the foolish obsession of redbits only?

The stream was beginning to dimple with gentle morning currents as Rensal reached the Tall One's house.

"Why do I care so much about beginnings?" asked Rensal. The Tall One was beginning to light his first pipe. "The stream doesn't seem to care a whit. It just flows and reflects me whenever I happen to be close to it," said Rensal indignantly.

"Oh, you can be sure you're still there, Rensal, even when it's not reflecting you," said the Tall One, trying to humor him, his pipe interrupting speech with punctuations of smoke.

"Oh, be serious," said Rensal. "At times I wish I were a stream that didn't have to care about where it came from."

"I thought you wanted to be a bird," said the Tall One, still teasing him.

"Oh, if you're not in a mood to be helpful, maybe I should look for answers in the stream," said Rensal, trying to direct his voice toward the water.

"I'm sorry," said the Tall One genuinely. "Beginnings are important." He chewed his pipe to emphasize what he was saying. "But middles and endings are important, too." He chewed again, punctuating speech with billows of smoke.

"Maybe you love beginnings because they take your mind off endings."

Truth was heavy in the air, a weight that gradually broke the silence.

"That still leaves middles," said Rensal, trying to avoid the logic of the issue.

"Middles are what we are made of, after all," said the Tall One. "Middles looking backwards and forwards always, at beginnings and endings." As the Tall One spoke, the wind went under a sapling's arm and wept a little.

"We are in the middle of a conversation about beginnings," laughed Rensal, finally becoming less serious.

"A conversation that should never have an ending," added the Tall One, looking at Rensal as the little one looked back at him, both of them beginning to understand what they were talking about.

As they talked, the ignorant sky went by many times in the middle of the stream with no beginning or end, it seemed, to its passing reflection.

XVI

One morning, Rensal awoke from a dream that troubled him so much he tried to stamp it out, like the cinders of a fire you have no further use of, but the dream refused to leave.

Rensal had a nagging memory. Dreams became a part of memory of course, a part he had grown to accept. But this dream he would have disowned if he knew how. The dream was set in a courtroom: a redbit judge was presiding; to his right a jury of redbits; in front of him a packed courtroom; the four walls resounding with the words, "No further questions."

Rensal awoke in a cold sweat. In an instant he knew what the dream meant. In an instant he knew what he was trying to forget. If he had no further questions for the Tall One … What a rotten peach of a thought.

Rensal walked around all day after this dream like a redbit who has eaten the berries that make you see things that are not really there at all. He hardly greeted Ludik and Silitar when they met. He hardly noticed the stream or the sky or the very grass he walked on. At times he was beside himself, leaning this way and that way into his thoughts.

"Have I grown tall, perhaps?" he asked himself. "Do tall ones run out of questions?" He ran to the stream and measured himself against time and memory in the stream as best he could. Certainly he was taller than when he had asked the Tall One the first question. But was he tall enough to be out of questions? He squeezed himself, hoping that a last question would drop into the stream and ripple endlessly.

"If I am taller, it means my shadow is longer. Small redbits will approach my shadow fearfully, the way I first greeted the Tall One. If I am taller, it means small redbits will question me the way I have pestered the Tall One. Will I be as kind and as wise as the Tall One? If I am taller, I will have to explain death and war to the little redbits the way the Tall One was brave enough to explain them to me."

Rensal looked in the stream again. He pretended at first that the image in the water was smaller than the one he really saw. "I am still Rensal," he said to himself, "Small as ever, full of questions."

It was a lie and he knew it. He walked towards the Tall One's house, kicking his shadow, hoping to knock a piece off it and make it smaller. What was the point of walking to the Tall One's house if he himself was a tall one already? "Let the Tall One walk to my house for a change," he thought to himself angrily. Rensal turned back, looked in the stream, went forward, turned back …

If Ludik and Silitar had seen him, they would have pointed at their temples, meaning that Rensal was out of his mind again! Eventually, Rensal reached the tall one's house.

"You're just in time for tea," said the Tall One.

"You and your tea," said Rensal rudely.

"What's the matter, Rensal?" asked the Tall One.

"Am I taller?" asked Rensal abruptly.

"Yes," said the Tall One honestly. "I have noticed lately that you are growing. What a wonder it is, growing."

"Some wonder," said Rensal, sulking. "Soon I'll have no questions," he added angrily.

"Rensal," said the Tall One, "I'll bet you had a dream in which the last question slipped off the edge of the world and you couldn't retrieve it."

"How do you know?" asked Rensal in amazement.

"Because I had a dream like that once. I was very frightened for a few days, until I realized there were many edges of the world and as soon as the last question fell off one edge, another edge appeared, waiting for another question to fall, believing itself to be the last."

Rensal smiled. "You mean even when I am as tall as you there will still be corners of the world for us to climb, even as our last questions fall off the edge?"

"Yes," said the Tall One, pouring tea. "And now, if you will permit me to have the last question: Would you like some berries with your toast?"

"Yes," said Rensal, relishing the last word.

ABOUT THE AUTHOR

Eugene J. Mahon, MD, is a Training and Supervising Analyst at the Columbia Psychoanalytic Center for Training and Research and at the Contemporary Freudian Society. He is also a member of the Center for Advanced Psychoanalytic Studies, Princeton, New Jersey. He won The Alexander Beller Award of Columbia Psychoanalytic Institute in 1984, and has been on the editorial boards of the *International Journal of Psychoanalysis*, the *Journal of The American Psychoanalytic Association* and he is currently on the editorial board of the *Psychoanalytic Quarterly*. He practices Child Analysis and Adult Analysis in New York City.